For Elizabeth and Amy Dale,
with love and fond memories of our Canadian
adventures searching for scary bears!
And for Louise Bolongaro,
with many thanks for her wonderful
vision and guidance.
E. D.

For my real-life Daddy Bear —John Nigel.
P. M.

Text copyright © 2016 by Elizabeth Dale
Illustrations copyright © 2016 by Paula Metcalf

Nosy Crow and its logos are trademarks of Nosy Crow Ltd.
Used under license.

First U.S. edition 2018

Library of Congress Catalog Card Number pending
ISBN 978-0-7636-9627-6

17 18 19 20 21 22 FGF 10 9 8 7 6 5 4 3 2 1

Printed in Shenzhen, Guangdong, China

This book was typeset in Baskerville.
The illustrations were done in mixed media.

Nosy Crow
an imprint of
Candlewick Press
99 Dover Street
Somerville, Massachusetts 02144

www.nosycrow.com
www.candlewick.com

Nothing Can Frighten a Bear

Elizabeth Dale illustrated by Paula Metcalf

nosy crow
An imprint of Candlewick Press

Deep, deep in the woods, with the moon shining bright,
some bears snuggled up in their beds for the night.

There was Mommy Bear, Daddy Bear . . .

Grace, and then Ben . . .

and Baby Bear, too,
who lay dreaming,
but then . . .

as Baby Bear jiggled
and wriggled some more,
he **suddenly** woke
when he heard a loud . . .

roar!

"Help!" Baby cried. "There's a monster about!
He's coming to get me — I just heard him shout."
"Don't worry," said Mommy Bear, stroking his head.
"There **aren't** any monsters. Let's go back to bed."

But Baby Bear whimpered, "How can you be **sure?**
I **can't** sleep till I know **what** made that big roar!"

"In that case," said Daddy Bear, grabbing a light,
"why don't we go looking for monsters **tonight?**

You'll see that there's nothing so scary out there.
And anyway, **nothing** can frighten a **bear!**"

So **five** bears went marching out through the tall trees
when Mom heard a noise and cried,
"Everyone—**freeze!**"

So all the bears stopped—could a **monster** be near?
But out of the darkness there trotted a . . . **deer!**

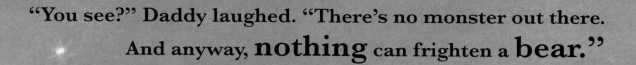

"You see?" Daddy laughed. "There's no monster out there.
And anyway, **nothing** can frighten a **bear.**"

The little bears said, "We're as **brave** as can be!"

But no one saw Mommy get caught in a . . .

tree!

So **four** bears went striding out into the night
when Ben saw a splash and squealed, "There! On our right!"
They stopped where they stood on a slippery log,
then out of the water there hopped a big . . . **frog!**

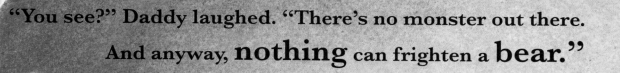

"You see?" Daddy laughed. "There's no monster out there.
And anyway, **nothing** can frighten a **bear**."

"Keep going," said Daddy. "There's no need to scream."
But no one saw Ben slip and fall in the . . .

stream!

So **three** bears squelched on down a thick, muddy track

when Grace said, "What's that? Something brushed past my back!"

"Perhaps it's a monster," said Baby. "Oh, no!"

But out of the darkness there swooped a black . . . **crow!**

"You see?" Daddy laughed. "There's no monster out there. And anyway, **nothing** can frighten a **bear.**"

They sploshed and they splashed as they tramped through the muck, but nobody noticed that Grace had got . . .

Now **two** bears were sleepily wandering on.
They **still** hadn't noticed the others had gone.
The lamp gave a flicker and started to fade.
"I want to go home," Baby said.
"I'm **afraid.**"

"All right, then," said Daddy, "let's get you to bed.
There aren't any monsters. It's just as I said!
I told you that **nothing** can frighten a **bear.**"
But then he looked round and saw . . .

nobody there!

"But **where** have the others gone?" Daddy Bear cried.
"I thought they were here, walking right by our side!
Perhaps they decided to go home to bed,
or . . . maybe a **monster** has got them instead!"

Then out of the darkness a **shadow** appeared.
"Oh, no!" Daddy cried. "This is worse than I feared!
Quick, take my paw, Baby, and hide behind me.
There isn't just **one** monster here. There are . . .

three!

Just look! They're so **fierce.**

How their scary eyes stare.

Now, **that** is a sight that can frighten a **bear.**

Oh, Baby"—he shuddered—
"we **must** run away!"
But just then the scariest monster roared . . .

"Hey!"

Poor Daddy Bear froze and cried,
"Baby, stay calm!"
But Baby Bear giggled and said,
"That's my **mom!**"

"You **sillies,**" said Mommy Bear. "Surely you see?
We may look a mess, but it's Ben, Grace, and me."
"It's you!" Daddy cried. "Oh, how silly I feel.
I thought for a second that monsters were **real.**"

So **five** bears went home, feeling ready for bed.

"We'll **all** stick together this time," Daddy said.

Deep, deep in the woods, with the moon shining bright, the bears snuggled up in their beds for the night.

Then **suddenly** everyone looked all around,
for **something** had just made a strange . . .

growly sound!

"I'm **sure** there's a monster now!" Baby Bear cried.

"No, Baby, it's **you!**" all the others replied.

"It wasn't a monster that scared you before.

You woke yourself up with your **own roary . . .**

snore!"